to Robinson Thoreau Stowell upstairs
with love from the outlaw downstairs! (MM)

for Ann Meo with love (HC)

also by Margaret Mahy and Helen Craig
JAM – a true story

First published 1990
Text © Margaret Mahy 1990
Illustrations © Helen Craig 1990

Jonathan Cape Ltd, 20 Vauxhall Bridge Road, London SW1V 2SA

A CIP catalogue record for this book
is available from the British Library

ISBN 0-224-02745-X

Printed in Great Britain by Cambus Litho, East Kilbride

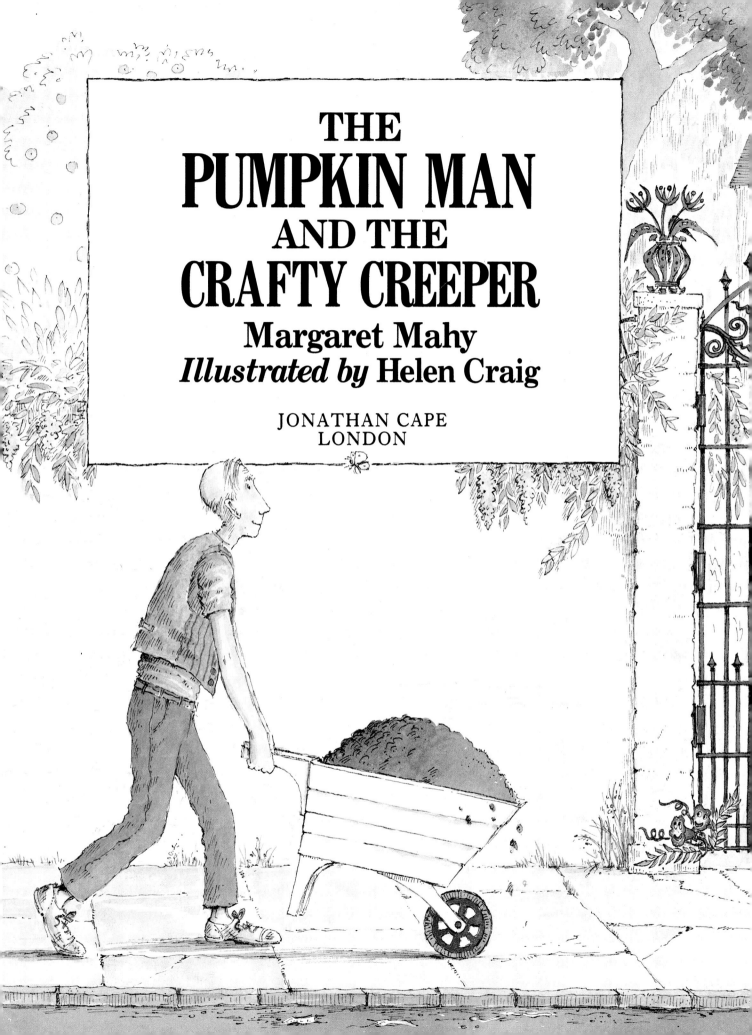

THE
PUMPKIN MAN
AND THE
CRAFTY CREEPER

Margaret Mahy
Illustrated by Helen Craig

JONATHAN CAPE
LONDON

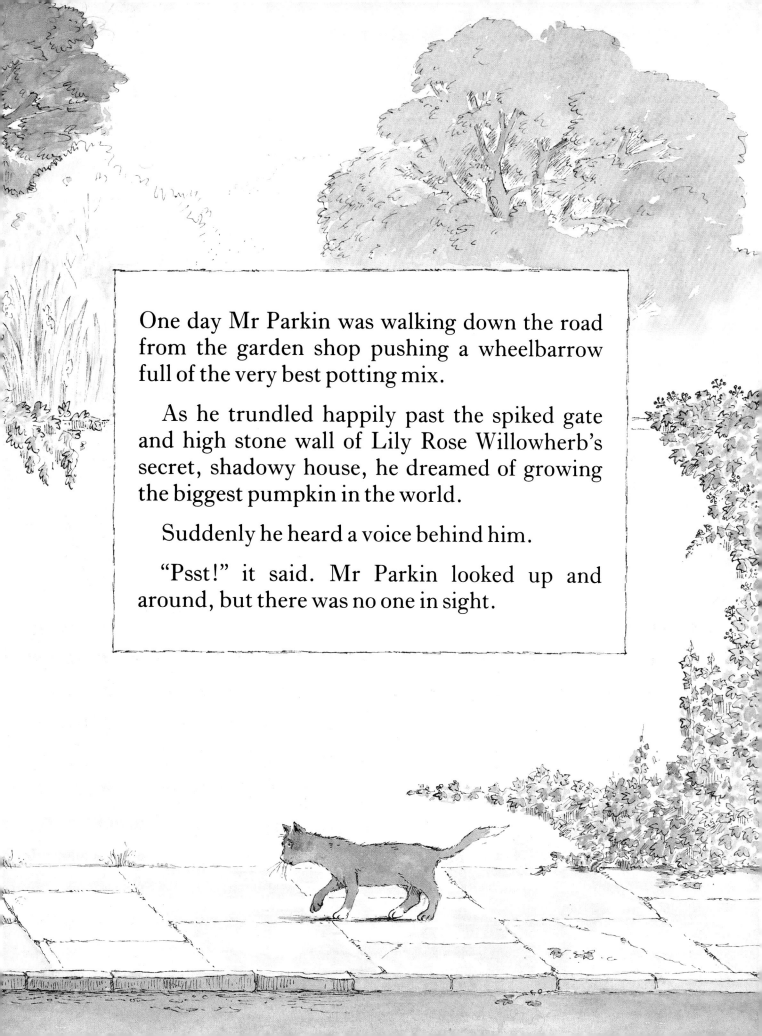

One day Mr Parkin was walking down the road from the garden shop pushing a wheelbarrow full of the very best potting mix.

As he trundled happily past the spiked gate and high stone wall of Lily Rose Willowherb's secret, shadowy house, he dreamed of growing the biggest pumpkin in the world.

Suddenly he heard a voice behind him.

"Psst!" it said. Mr Parkin looked up and around, but there was no one in sight.

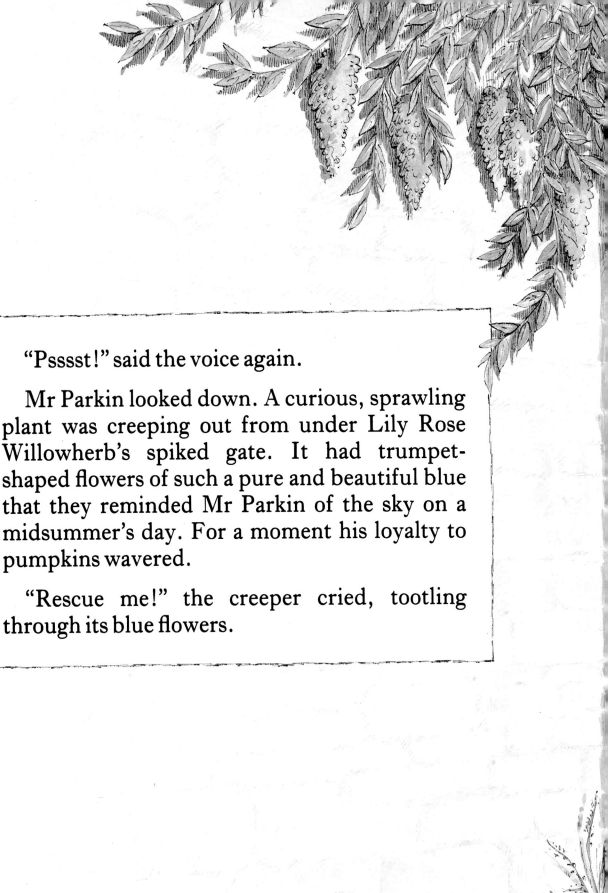

"Psssst!" said the voice again.

Mr Parkin looked down. A curious, sprawling plant was creeping out from under Lily Rose Willowherb's spiked gate. It had trumpet-shaped flowers of such a pure and beautiful blue that they reminded Mr Parkin of the sky on a midsummer's day. For a moment his loyalty to pumpkins wavered.

"Rescue me!" the creeper cried, tootling through its blue flowers.

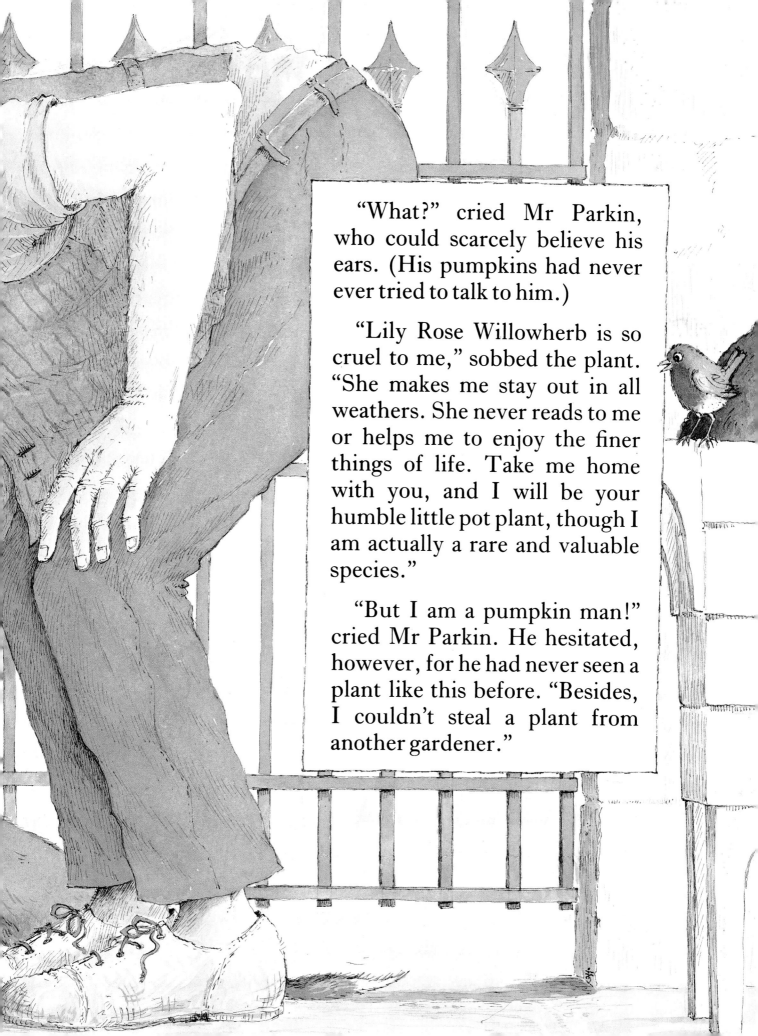

"What?" cried Mr Parkin, who could scarcely believe his ears. (His pumpkins had never ever tried to talk to him.)

"Lily Rose Willowherb is so cruel to me," sobbed the plant. "She makes me stay out in all weathers. She never reads to me or helps me to enjoy the finer things of life. Take me home with you, and I will be your humble little pot plant, though I am actually a rare and valuable species."

"But I am a pumpkin man!" cried Mr Parkin. He hesitated, however, for he had never seen a plant like this before. "Besides, I couldn't steal a plant from another gardener."

"No, of course not!" said the plant. "Luckily, I am a creeper. You pretend to do up your shoe-laces, and I'll creepy-creep-creep myself into your wheelbarrow."

Mr Parkin was tempted. While he pretended to do up his shoe-laces, the creeper crept into his wheelbarrow and burrowed under the potting mix.

Mr Parkin took it home and planted it in a nice large pot.

"How about a sprinkle of water?" asked the plant.

"I'm coming to that," Mr Parkin said. He sprinkled the plant with plenty of water.

"More!" demanded the plant. Mr Parkin sprinkled it again.

"Oh dear. I'm afraid that's a bit too much," said the plant rather crossly.

"Well, it will soon soak in," said Mr Parkin, dismayed by the plant's lack of gratitude.

"I'm all soggy about the roots," the plant grumbled. Mr Parkin hated grumblers.

"I must go and water my pumpkins," he said sternly.

"Just turn on the television before you go out," the plant ordered in a bossy voice.

"I don't have a television," snapped Mr Parkin.

"What?" cried the plant. "No television! Why didn't you mention that before you forced me to creepy-creep-creep into your wheelbarrow?"

"You didn't ask me!" Mr Parkin was beginning to feel impatient with this provoking plant.

"I must have entertainment," the plant moaned. "I need the finer things of life. Look, I'm beginning to droop. I shall die. I shall die!"

It was true. The plant really was beginning to droop.

Hastily, Mr Parkin dashed into his bedroom, grabbed his trusty banjo, and dashed back again. He began to strum madly and sing a jolly song.

"If you could just do a little dance as well, I might feel better," the plant said in a small, weak voice. Mr Parkin obligingly played on the banjo while kicking up his long, thin legs.

The plant quickly revived and began tootling through its trumpet-shaped flowers, swaying its leaves in time to the music.

"Look, I *must* run out and water my pumpkins," Mr Parkin said.

"Oh, I can't bear it," the plant wept. "I need music, poetry, light and laughter. Is that too much to ask?"

Mr Parkin ran and looked up 'Entertainment' in the yellow pages of the telephone directory. *Dial-an-orchestra!* said one advertisement. *Fill your home with beautiful music, day and night.*

Mr Parkin hastily rang the number. "What do you advise for a sensitive plant that needs music, poetry, light and laughter?" he cried into the phone.

"We recommend a full symphony orchestra!" replied the dial-an-orchestra man.

"We will rush our best orchestra round to you at once. The musicians will bring their own strawberries, but we ask our clients to provide the champagne."

"Strawberries? Champagne?" shrieked Mr Parkin.

"They have to eat, you know," said the dial-an-orchestra man. "Playing violins and tubas and things is extremely hard work. Do you have your own grand piano?"

"I have a trusty banjo," Mr Parkin answered.

"Oh, that is not at all the same thing," answered the dial-an-orchestra man. "We'll do the best we can, but I can't guarantee perfect results without a piano."

There was scarcely any room for the orchestra in Mr Parkin's kitchen. The musicians had to stand on chairs and sit on top of the fridge. At last, however, they were all settled.

"I'm looking forward to this," said the plant.

As the orchestra began to play, Mr Parkin slipped outside to water his pumpkins.

Wonderful music began to drift out over the garden. People gathered at Mr Parkin's gate to listen. Even the pumpkins began to sway in time to the music.

When Mr Parkin tried to make a cup of tea in his overcrowded kitchen a particularly vigorous trombone player sent his cup shooting right off the saucer, through the window and into the pumpkins outside. However, Mr Parkin did not complain as the plant was clearly happy listening to the music.

The orchestra played mightily, sustaining itself with strawberries and champagne in between minuets and mazurkas.

"How about some poetry?" the plant called when it suddenly caught sight of Mr Parkin. "Forget those pumpkins. Read me some poetry."

"Forget my pumpkins!" cried Mr Parkin indignantly. "Never!"

"I shall die without poetry," declared the plant dramatically, beginning to droop on purpose. But at that moment the door opened and who should come in but Lily Rose Willowherb herself, wearing her coat of many colours and her red high-heeled shoes. The plant tried to hide behind the curtains as soon as it saw her, but it was not quick enough.

"You wretched plant!" cried Lily Rose Willowherb. "The moment I heard that orchestra I guessed just where you were."

"He kidnapped me! He kidnapped me!" cried the treacherous plant in a panic. "He reached through the gate and dragged me into his wheelbarrow."

"What a lot of rubbish you talk!" muttered Lily Rose Willowherb. To Mr Parkin she said, "You should never, ever take any notice of anything this plant says. It is well known for being treacherous and ungrateful."

"I'm too sensitive for this rough life," wept the plant. "I'm beginning to droop."

"You? Droop? You're as tough as old boots," said Lily Rose Willowherb, whisking it out of its pot. "You're so tough you're practically a weed."

"A weed!" cried the plant in horror, and it pretended to faint.

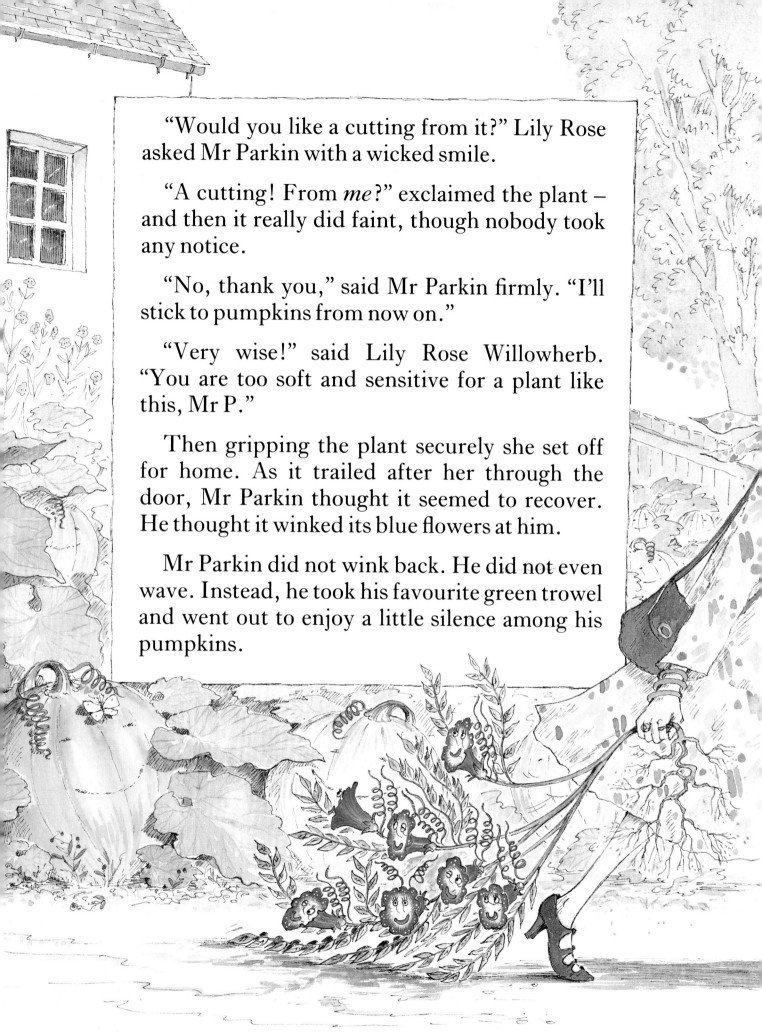

"Would you like a cutting from it?" Lily Rose asked Mr Parkin with a wicked smile.

"A cutting! From *me*?" exclaimed the plant – and then it really did faint, though nobody took any notice.

"No, thank you," said Mr Parkin firmly. "I'll stick to pumpkins from now on."

"Very wise!" said Lily Rose Willowherb. "You are too soft and sensitive for a plant like this, Mr P."

Then gripping the plant securely she set off for home. As it trailed after her through the door, Mr Parkin thought it seemed to recover. He thought it winked its blue flowers at him.

Mr Parkin did not wink back. He did not even wave. Instead, he took his favourite green trowel and went out to enjoy a little silence among his pumpkins.